WOKE BABY

MAHOGANY L. BROWNE

ILLUSTRATED BY **THEODORE TAYLOR III**

ROARING BROOK PRESS

NEW YORK

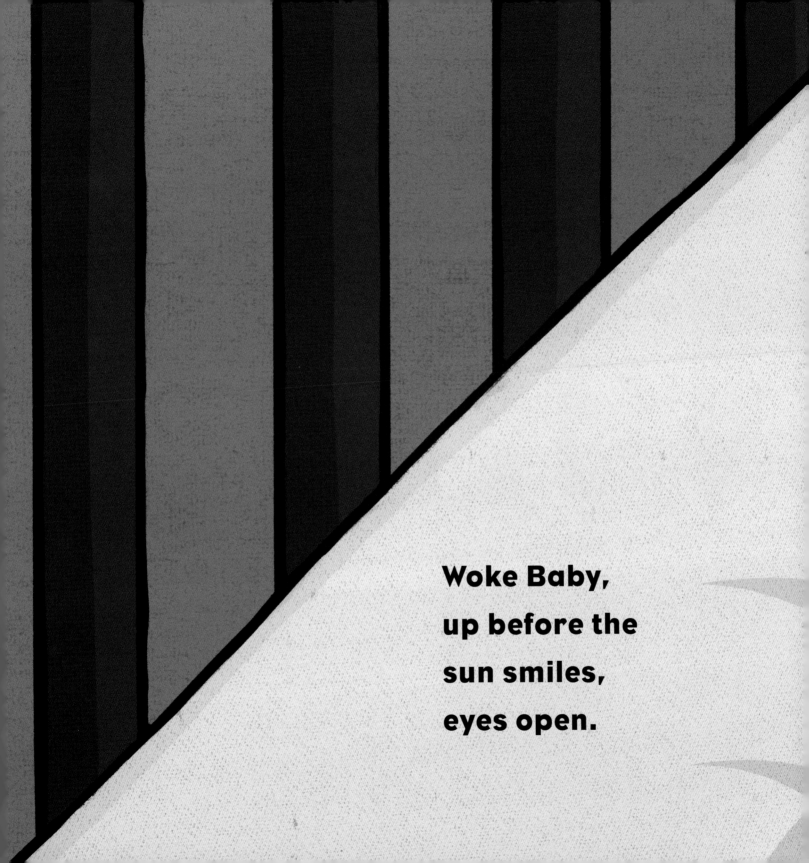

Woke Baby,
up before the
sun smiles,
eyes open.

Look at your fists,
fingers curled
into a panther's paw
pointing up up up,
reaching for justice.

Look at each toe,
wiggling hello to the sky.
There is no glass ceiling,
there is no one to tell you no!

Up up up on each knee,
bent like half-moons.
Woke Baby,
you are an awakened
dream.

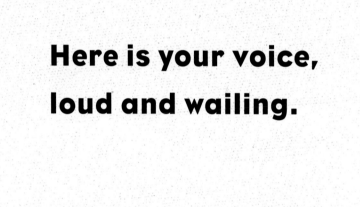

Here is your voice,
loud and wailing.

Here are your hands,
reaching for what
is yours.

**Here are your eyes,
widened and bright.**

**Woke Baby,
you stop for no one.**

**You twist to your own beat,
you babble songs of freedom.**

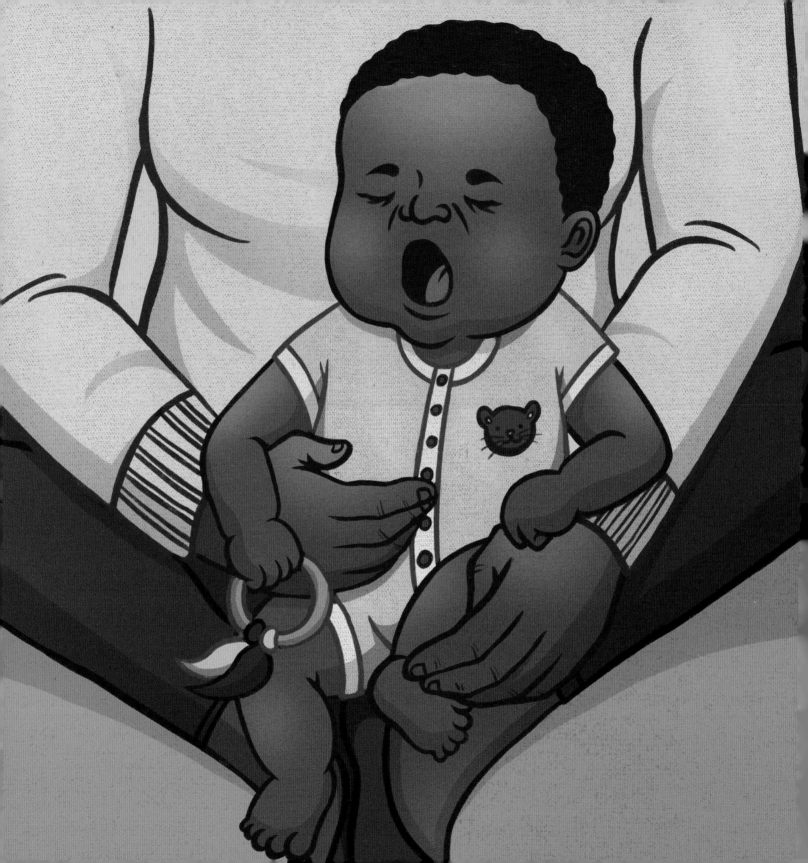

**Like a good revolutionary,
you never, ever sleep.**

Only rest,
only rest,
until the next dawn.

**To those raising and teaching our babies
to stay woke and to rise** —M. B.

To my son, Theo. Stay woke! —T. T.

Text copyright © 2018 by Mahogany L. Browne
Illustrations copyright © 2018 by Theodore Taylor III

Published by Roaring Brook Press
Roaring Brook Press is a division of Holtzbrinck Publishing Holdings Limited Partnership
175 Fifth Avenue, New York, NY 10010

mackids.com

Library of Congress Control Number: 2018944886
ISBN: 978-1-62672-295-8

Our books may be purchased in bulk for promotional, educational, or business use. Please contact your local
bookseller or the Macmillan Corporate and Premium Sales Department at (800) 221-7945 ext. 5442 or by email
at MacmillanSpecialMarkets@macmillan.com.

First edition, 2018
Book design by Monique Sterling
Printed in China by RR Donnelley Asia Printing Solutions Ltd., Dongguan City, Guangdong Province

1 3 5 7 9 10 8 6 4 2